Printed in the United States of America.
Published in Indianapolis by
Script Novel Publishing.
First Printing, 2021

Contact: www.TravisPeagler.com,
via TravisWriter@TravisPeagler.com

Book Cover Design by: Blueberry Illustrations

ueberry Illustrations is a world class illustrations and
elf publishing company. The illustrators of Blueberry
rations are recipients of various awards and nominations.
e than 1500 books have been illustrated and published
by the company and many more are in the making.

www.blueberryillustrations.com

ISBN: 9781732563551

Library of Congress Control Number: 2021901239

Bizzy Bzz the Bee
Grandpa's

Travis Peagler

Illustrations by Blueberry Illustra

Illus
M

Bizzy Bzzz the Bee and Grandpa's Tea

is reading made fun. Told through the eyes of a child, this is an entertaining story about a boy who gets a good laugh watching Grandpa's encounter with a bee every morning while trying to enjoy his cup of tea. Teetering on the edge of frustration, Grandpa has a heightened escalation with Bizzy.

The boy comes up with a quick solution that allows Grandpa to enjoy his morning tea and lets Bizzy stay. It's safe to say, the Grandson saved the day. This story has playful rhyme, problem solving, and is sure to put a smile on faces of children every time.

Every morning at seven o' three,
I wake up just in time to watch
Grandpa play with Bizzy Bzzz the Bee.

First Grandpa puts in his pretend
teeth before anyone can see...

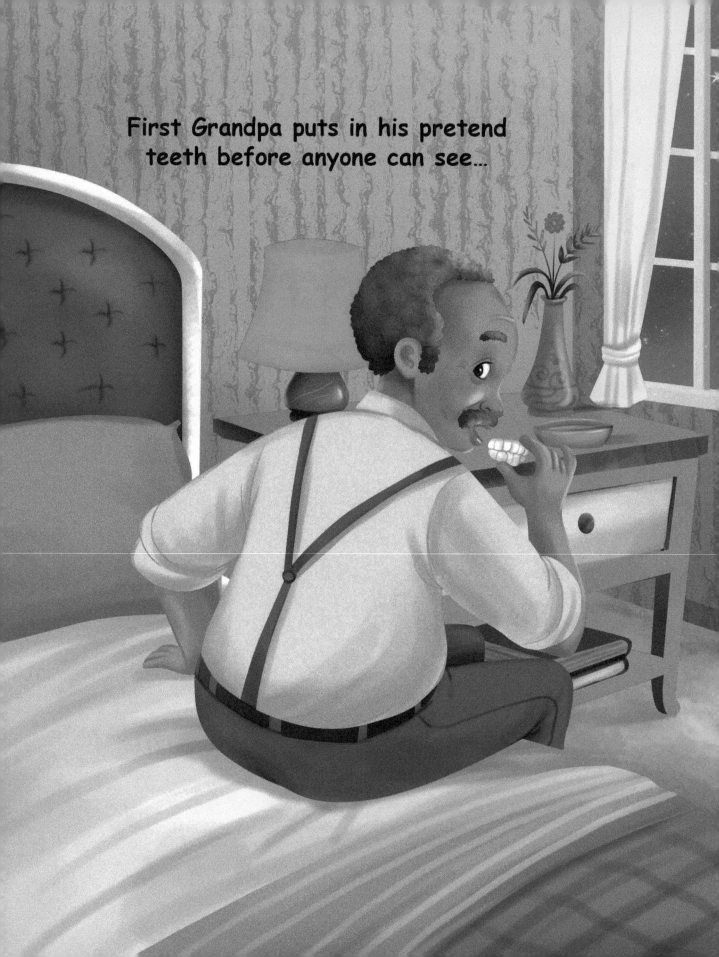

he kneels to pray and then turns on the TV. I don't think, wink, wink that Grandpa can talk to God without his special teeth.

Then he stretches his back—
he feels much better after the
creaks, pops, and cracks!

His dog, Sparks, is happy to greet him with a wet licking kiss that Grandpa never seems to miss.

Grandpa hurries into the kitchen to make his tea.
He does not want to miss the sunrise, you see.

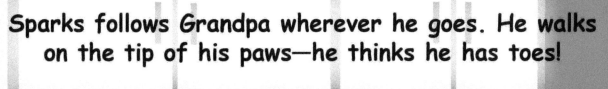

Sparks follows Grandpa wherever he goes. He walks on the tip of his paws—he thinks he has toes!

Now it's off to the porch, where there's much to see, and tea to sip, when suddenly a bee zips past Grandpa's lip.

Every morning at twilight, when I hear the buzzing sound, bzzz, bzzz, I know it's time for Gramps to fight! Grandpa does a running dance as if he has ants in his pants!

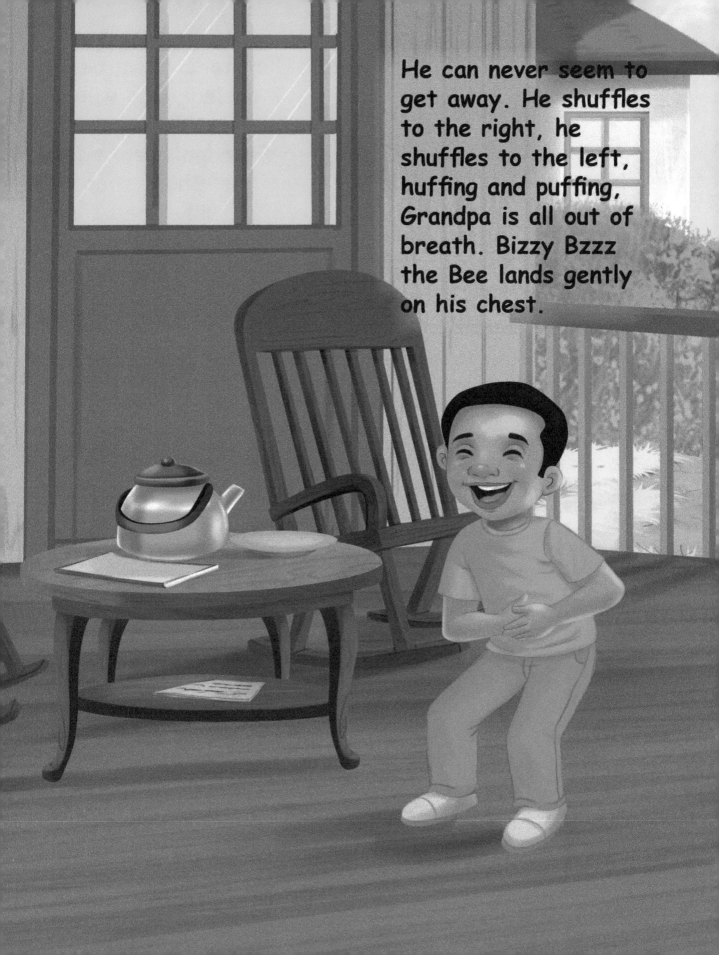

He can never seem to get away. He shuffles to the right, he shuffles to the left, huffing and puffing, Grandpa is all out of breath. Bizzy Bzzz the Bee lands gently on his chest.

"I blow and blow, I shoo with my fist, but somehow, I always seem to miss. I love the sunrise, and I love the morning dew, please, you little old bee, just let me be." Bizzy Bzzz zips around Grandpa's head three times and makes him dizzy. It's funny when his eyes cross. He looks so silly.

Grandpa stumbles back and slips. "Oh no!" I yell. "C'mon, Sparks, catch Grandpa so he doesn't bust his rump on the ground, and I'll catch the cup of tea before it crashes with a loud sound." Like two

heroes in action, we
stop bad things from happenin'.
I race over fast and catch the
glass, as if I were catching a pass.
Before Grandpa falls flat, Sparks rushes
behind him so he can land on his back.

"Ahhh, what would I do, without the two of you,"
says Grandpa. "Y'all saved my bacon, I was scared,
heart-pounding, and my hands were shakin'."
Grandpa was pleased to see I didn't spill a single
drop of tea. With all the ruckus, Bizzy Bzzz
flew away, but I knew he'd be back to play.

Grandpa finally takes a sip of tea... and
what's that we see? It's Bizzy Bzzz the Bee.
He's back for round two and three.
"He's just lonely, Grandpa,
or maybe he's hungry," I say.
"Oh no, a little peace
and quiet is all I ask."
"I got a great idea, Grandpa,
finally—at last."

I hurry into the house to find the smallest glass, fill it with tea, and a teaspoon of honey.

Back outside,
we can hardly
wait to see,
Bizzy Bzzz,
that crazy bee,
heads straight
for the honey!

"A-ha, you smart boy, it has finally dawned on me why this bee was chasing me! Well, now I see, it wasn't me he was after, but the honey in my tea."

"Now, this old man has a new best friend, besides my super grandson and my dog, Sparks, who loves to bark. Blessed is the morning the Lord has made for you and me, I'm so happy to share it with Bizzy Bzzz the Bee, along with two cups of tea!"

A Special Poem for You

"Dear Child"

The morning breeze awakes you, the butterflies tickle you...
as the sun shines bright and smiles down on you. The wind
carries you. The lily flowers smell deliciously sweet as
the bumblebees bring honey for your tiny tummy. All the way,
at the end of your playful day, the moon kisses you Goodnight...

Travis Peagler is a unique individual,

being the youngest of seven kids, raised partially in low-income apartments on the East side of Dayton, Ohio, until the age of nine. Humble beginnings growing up in a somewhat multi-racial neighborhood gave Travis an inimitable perspective on life at an incredibly young age.

His imagination has always been his outlet. Thinking back to grade-school when he was in an uncomfortable situation or when he didn't handle conflict well, Travis would always replay the scene again in his mind where things played out the way he wished. An innate defense mechanism, he assumes, which led to the discovery of his extraordinary talent.

Stay in touch with Travis for other and future books at:

www.TravisPeagler.com
Email: TravisWriter@TravisPeagler.com
Facebook: @ScriptNovels
Instagram: @TravisWriterPeagler
Follow him at amazon.com/author/travispeagler

CPSIA information can be obtained
at www.ICGtesting.com
Printed in the USA
LVHW071802100521
687011LV00007B/199